EARTHQUAKES

MICHAEL GEORGE

CREATIVE EDUCATION

Designed by Rita Marshall
with the help of Melinda Belter

Published by Creative Education,
123 South Broad Street, Mankato,
Minnesota 56001.

Creative Education is an imprint of
The Creative Company

Photography by Comstock, F-Stock,
Gerry Ellis, Peter Arnold Inc., and
Photo Researchers

Library of Congress

Cataloging-in-Publication Data

George, Michael, 1964 -

Earthquakes / Michael George.

   p.   cm.
ISBN 0-88682-709-4
1. Earthquakes–Juvenile literature.
[1. Earthquakes.]   I. Title.
93-46806
QE521.3.G45   1997   CIP
551.2'2–dc20   AC

5 4 3 2 1

Printed in Hong Kong

7

On October 17, 1989, the eyes of the world were on San Francisco for the third game of the World Series. Shortly before the first pitch, the stadium began to quiver, and the restless crowd inside it grew still. Outside the stadium, the ground started to rumble, wobble, and heave. Across the city, people watched in terror as highways collapsed, buildings crumbled, and fires raged. On this historic night in San Francisco, there were no strikeouts, double plays, or home runs by the teams. Instead, there was horror and destruction, inflicted by the Great Quake of 1989.

San Francisco earthquake aftermath.

Earthquakes have intrigued and terrified us since our ancient ancestors first roamed the earth. In an attempt to understand these unpredictable and frightening events, primitive people dreamed up bizarre explanations for earthquakes. Ancient myths, for example, told of monsters that lived under the ground and supported the surface of the earth. When angered or restless, the creatures would shake the ground and cause an earthquake.

Today, *Seismologists*, scientists who study earthquakes, know that earthquakes are caused by the same forces that create mountain ranges and produce volcanic eruptions. Earthquakes are a natural result of the processes that make the earth a beautiful, ever-changing planet.

Upthrusting at the Colorado Plateau in Utah.

To understand what causes earthquakes, we must look deep inside our planet. The earth is made up of several distinct layers, each with different characteristics. The relatively thin covering of soil and rock on which we stand, the outermost layer of the earth, is called the *Crust*. Beneath the crust is the *Mantle*, a layer of hot, liquid rock. Deeper still is the earth's inner *Core*, which is a densely packed ball of iron, squeezed tightly together under the weight of the planet.

Although it feels as if the ground beneath our feet is solid and secure, the earth's crust is not as permanent or stable as we may think. Cracked like ancient pottery, the crust is divided into approximately twenty large pieces called *Tectonic Plates*. The plates are

constantly moving, driven by currents that roll up from the planet's hot, seething interior. Ever so slowly, the various plates drift apart, crash together, and grind against each other.

Along some plate boundaries, the plates crash head-on and buckle under the tremendous force of the collision. As the plates slowly crush together, the land heaves upward and forms great mountain ranges. Along other plate boundaries, one plate may slide beneath the other and melt as it sinks into the earth's hot interior. Sometimes this molten material rises through cracks in the earth's crust to escape in a volcanic eruption.

North American and European tectonic plates meet in Iceland.

Tectonic plates can also slide along their common boundaries. A fracture in the earth's crust where two plates slide past each other is called a *Fault*. Most faults lie far beneath the ground, but some faults, such as the San Andreas Fault in California, are visible on the earth's surface.

Movement along a fault is not a continuous process. The plates are jammed together so tightly that friction usually prevents them from moving. Over many years, stress slowly builds up along the fault as the plates try to grind past each other. Eventually, the pressure becomes too great and the plates finally slip with a jerk. This jerk is an earthquake.

When a fault slips, earthshaking vibrations called *Seismic Waves* travel through the ground much like waves of water travel through the ocean. Seismic waves are strongest where the fault actually slips. This region, called the earthquake's *Focus*, is usually located underground. On the earth's surface, the strongest seismic waves are felt above the focus, at the *Epicenter*.

Pressure ridges formed due to fault movements.

Earthquakes vary greatly in intensity. Seismologists use a system called the *Richter Scale* to measure the intensity of an earthquake. Each value on the Richter scale represents an earthquake that is ten times stronger than one of the next lower magnitude. For example, an earthquake that measures 7.0 on the Richter scale is 10 times stronger than one that measures 6.0, and 100 times stronger than one that measures 5.0.

Every day, all over the world, more than 1,000 earthquakes occur that measure less than 5.0 on the Richter scale. Seismologists consider these earthquakes minor because they rarely cause serious damage. Such earthquakes often go unnoticed or are mistaken for the passing of a large truck.

Earthquakes larger than 7.0 on the Richter scale, on the other hand, cannot be overlooked. These major earthquakes can move mountains and level cities. Fortunately, major earthquakes occur less frequently than smaller ones because it takes longer to build up sufficient stress. A major earthquake takes place somewhere about once a week. Even this is not as alarming as it sounds, since most major earthquakes occur on the ocean floor or in sparsely inhabited areas.

A coral reef is exposed when an earthquake raises the coastline six inches.

When a major earthquake does strike a populated area, it is capable of causing severe damage. Near the epicenter of a major earthquake, seismic waves wreak havoc on the normally solid surface of the earth. Streets roll with sweeping waves, trees bend to touch the ground, and buildings collapse like houses of cards. The momentary shaking of the ground may also cause massive landslides or avalanches. These sweeping rivers of land or snow can bury entire towns. Major earthquakes may also be followed by devastating floods, caused when natural or man-made dams are damaged by the shaking ground.

Accompanying these startling sights are the unique and terrifying sounds of an earthquake. Deeper and more disturbing than the rumbling of thunder, the sounds of an earthquake are felt as much as they are heard. Mixed with the constant growl are more recognizable sounds of destruction: snapping wood, crashing bricks, and shattering glass.

The Regis Hotel in ruins after a quake in Mexico City.

After the upheaval of a large earthquake, the continuing adjustment of the earth's crust often produces smaller tremors called *Aftershocks.* Some aftershocks are nearly as big as the major quake. Although most aftershocks are much lower on the Richter scale, they can cause serious damage by triggering the collapse of buildings, roads, and bridges already weakened by the major quake. Aftershocks may occur hours, days, weeks, or even months after a quake, usually becoming lesser in size and frequency.

On rare occasions, a major earthquake is preceded by small quakes called *Foreshocks.* Scientists cannot always tell whether mild quakes are announcements of a large quake coming or simply an adjustment of pressure on the earth's plates.

Earthquakes can gradually alter the landscape.

On April 18, 1906, one of the most famous earthquakes in history shook San Francisco, California. Although the quake lasted less than one minute, the momentary shaking overturned gas stoves and severed gas mains. The resulting fires raged unchecked throughout the city. After it was all over, 700 people had died and 300,000 had lost their homes. Most of the city, including 28,000 buildings, was destroyed.

The 1906 San Francisco earthquake was one of the worst catastrophes in the history of the United States, but earthquakes in other countries have been far more disastrous. The deadliest earthquake in recorded history occurred in China in the year 1566. Although precise accounts are not available, historians estimate that 830,000 people died. More recently, in 1976, an earthquake measuring 7.8 on the Richter scale hit Tangshan, China. In a matter of seconds, the modern industrial city of one million people was reduced to rubble. More than 240,000 people perished.

A marina fire in the aftermath of the 1989 San Francisco quake.

Earthquakes don't have to occur on land to cause terrible destruction. When an earthquake occurs under the ocean, the movement of the seafloor can give the water a sudden push, creating a dangerous wave called a *Tsunami*, or tidal wave.

Once generated, a tsunami can travel thousands of miles. In the open ocean, a tsunami is harmless and can often pass ships with no notice. However, when a tsunami enters shallow water near a coast, the wave crest can become as tall as a ten-story building. When the wall of water crashes onto land, it destroys nearly everything in its path. The coastline may remain underwater for 15 minutes or more, until the water is drawn back out to sea. The retreating water rips loose anything that has not yet been displaced. Smaller and smaller waves often follow the initial rush of water and complete the destruction.

Tidal wave created by an underwater earthquake.

Fortunately, scientists can usually locate and track a tsunami long before it reaches land, giving coastal inhabitants time to evacuate the threatened area. Earthquakes, on the other hand, strike without warning, and there is no accurate way to predict where or when the next one will occur. However, if a fault has generated a big earthquake in the past, it can be assumed that it will probably do so again. Southern California, for instance, can expect a major earthquake at least once every 50 to 100 years.

Los Angeles has experienced many earthquakes.

25

Although short-term warnings are not possible, precautionary measures can be taken to save lives and reduce damage in areas at high risk for earthquakes. Buildings, bridges, and roads can be constructed with special reinforcement techniques that minimize damage. Gas lines and water mains can be equipped with flexible joints that allow the pipes to stretch and compress during a quake, preventing gas leaks and water damage. Ultimately, however, there is no way to completely safeguard a city from destruction in the event of a major earthquake.

People who live in areas prone to earthquakes should be informed about what to do when an earthquake hits. Indoors, it's best to seek shelter from falling debris by getting under a sturdy table, desk, or bed, or by standing in a doorway. Windows should be avoided, and candles or matches should be extinguished. Outside, people should move away from buildings and overhead electrical wires. The safest outdoor location in a city is the middle of a wide street. People who are in a car when an earthquake begins should come to a stop but remain in the vehicle.

Page 26: Landsliding near San Francisco.
Page 27: Los Angeles highway interrupted.

While precautionary steps can limit the damage caused by earthquakes, scientists may someday be able to prevent catastrophic earthquakes altogether. One of the most promising methods for preventing earthquakes was discovered by accident in 1966, when millions of tons of fluid waste were buried deep beneath the ground in Colorado.

Shortly after the dumping began, a series of small tremors shook the area. When the disposal was stopped, the tremors also ceased. After researching this strange series of events, scientists determined that the fluid was lubricating an underground fault, making it easier for the fault to slip.

A collapsed bridge in Oakland.

By periodically causing *Controlled Earth-quakes*, seismologists may be able to relieve stress along a fault and prevent sudden, catastrophic earthquakes. Although this technique seems promising, more research is needed before the method can be used. Seismologists have not yet determined how neighboring faults interact, and any mistake could be disastrous.

San Andreas Fault.

Long before we began dreaming of ways to control earthquakes, our ancestors imagined that treacherous creatures were responsible for shaking the ground. Although *Earthquakes* still evoke terror, we now have a better understanding of why they occur. With this understanding, we can reduce the devastation that they cause and better appreciate the hidden forces that make our world a beautiful, living planet.

Index